COMMUNITY LIBRARY ASSN.
KETCHUM, ID 83340

COMMUNITY LIBRARY ASSN.
KETCHUM, ID 83340

THE MEAN HYENA
A FOLKTALE FROM MALAWI

Retold by
JUDY SIERRA

Illustrated by
MICHAEL BRYANT

Dutton LODESTAR BOOKS New York

Text copyright ©1997 by Judy Sierra
Illustrations copyright ©1997 by Michael Bryant

All rights reserved.

Library of Congress Cataloging-in-Publication Data
Sierra, Judy
The mean hyena: a folktale from Malawi / retold by Judy Sierra;
illustrated by Michael Bryant
p. cm.
Summary: After suffering as a victim of one of Fisi the hyena's nasty
tricks, Kamba the tortoise offers to paint new coats for all the animals
as a way of getting revenge on Fisi.
ISBN 0-525-67510-8 (alk. paper)
[1. Folklore—Malawi. 2. Animals—Folklore.]
I. Bryant, Michael, ill. II. Title
PZ8.1.S573Me 1997
398.2′096897′0452792—dc20
[E] 96-349 CIP AC

Published in the United States by Lodestar Books,
an affiliate of Dutton Children's Books,
a member of Penguin Putnam Inc.
375 Hudson Street, New York, New York 10014

Published simultaneously in Canada
by McClelland & Stewart, Toronto

Editor: Virginia Buckley   Designer: Dick Granald

Printed in Hong Kong   First Edition
10 9 8 7 6 5 4 3 2 1

To Mickey Aronoff

J.S.

To James and Lesa Ransome.

May the kindness that you spread be given to

you and your children.

Thanks for your influence on my career.

M.B.

Tell me! Who is this? He thinks
his vest is so fine he never takes it off,
even when he sleeps.

Kamba! The tortoise!

One evening, Kamba was walking along
a path in the tall, dry grass.

Sniff, trot, sniff, trot. Here comes Fisi the hyena,
the big troublemaker.

"Eh! Kamba! Want to go for a ride, eh?
Want to fly to the sky, eh?" asked the hyena.

"No, thank you," answered the tortoise.
He knew about Fisi's nasty tricks.

The hyena lowered his head, picked
up the tortoise with his mouth, and walked over
to a tree. He pushed Kamba's shell between
two branches and left him there, stuck tight.

The hyena danced away, barking
and laughing, "Ha, ha, ha! Ha, ha, ha!"

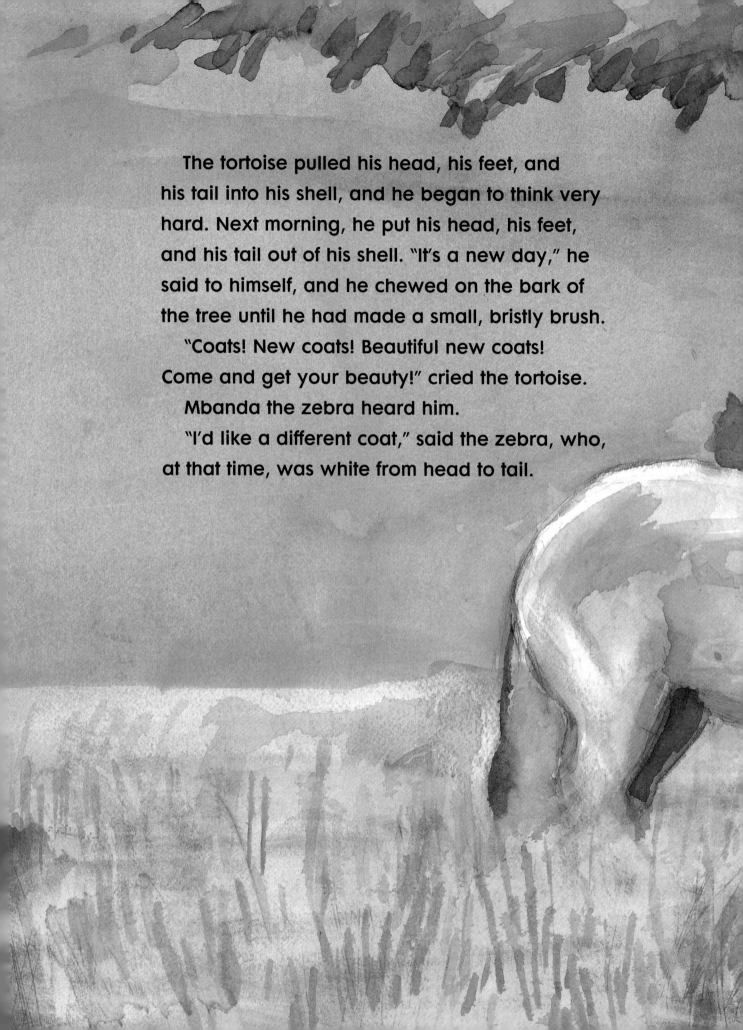

The tortoise pulled his head, his feet, and his tail into his shell, and he began to think very hard. Next morning, he put his head, his feet, and his tail out of his shell. "It's a new day," he said to himself, and he chewed on the bark of the tree until he had made a small, bristly brush.

"Coats! New coats! Beautiful new coats! Come and get your beauty!" cried the tortoise.

Mbanda the zebra heard him.

"I'd like a different coat," said the zebra, who, at that time, was white from head to tail.

The tortoise looked at the zebra. "Yes," he said, "you will be very beautiful. Bring black dye, lots of it."

The zebra brought black dye, and the tortoise began—slowly, carefully—to make long, flowing stripes on Mbanda's coat. The zebra turned this way and that way so the tortoise could paint her everywhere.

Now, until that time, the zebra had lived in the village, like her cousin the horse. But the zebra's new coat was so lovely that people wanted to touch her all the time. This annoyed the zebra, and she ran away into the wild country. She has stayed there ever since.

"Coats! New coats! Beautiful
new coats! Come and get your beauty!"
cried the tortoise again.

Nyalugwe the leopard was tired
of his plain yellow coat, and so he went
to see the tortoise in the tree.

"Please, could you paint my coat?"
asked the leopard. "But don't give
me stripes, or else the zebra will think
I copied her."

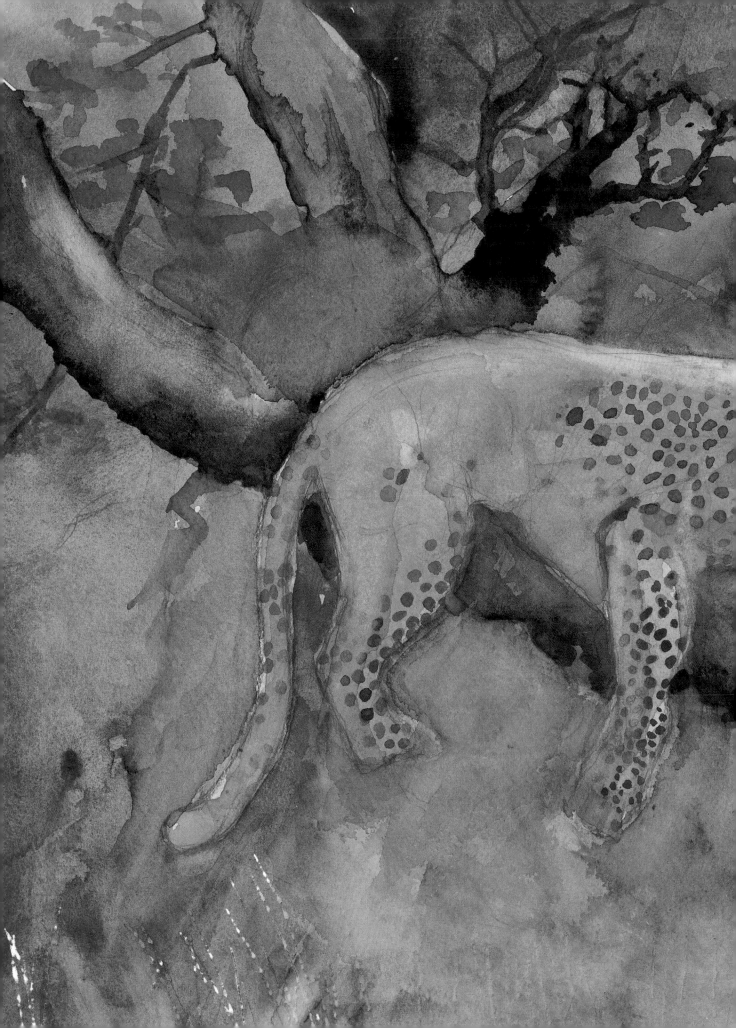

The tortoise told the leopard to bring
him some brown dye. Then Nyalugwe stretched
out on a branch of the tree, rolling this way
and that way as the tortoise painted spots of
many shapes and sizes on his coat.

Now, until this time, the leopard had lived
in the village, like his smaller cousin the cat. But
the people of the village loved the leopard's
new coat so much that they were always
stroking and petting him. This bothered the
leopard, and he, too, went to live in the wild
country, where he still lives today.

"Coats! New coats! Beautiful new coats! Come and get your beauty!" Animals lined up beneath the tree to receive new colors and designs from the tortoise.

Finally, night-skulking Fisi heard about Kamba's wonderful coat painting. The hyena was quite proud of his smooth, brown coat, but it seemed dull compared to Mbanda's and Nyalugwe's. So he went to see the tortoise in the tree.

"Eh! Give me my beauty!" he demanded.

"First, help me get down from here," said the tortoise.

The hyena took the tortoise in his mouth and gently lowered him to the ground.

"Now, bring sticky tree gum," said the tortoise. "The more the better."

Fisi soon returned with a bowl of tree gum. The tortoise cheerfully dabbed globs and splots of gum onto the hyena's coat.

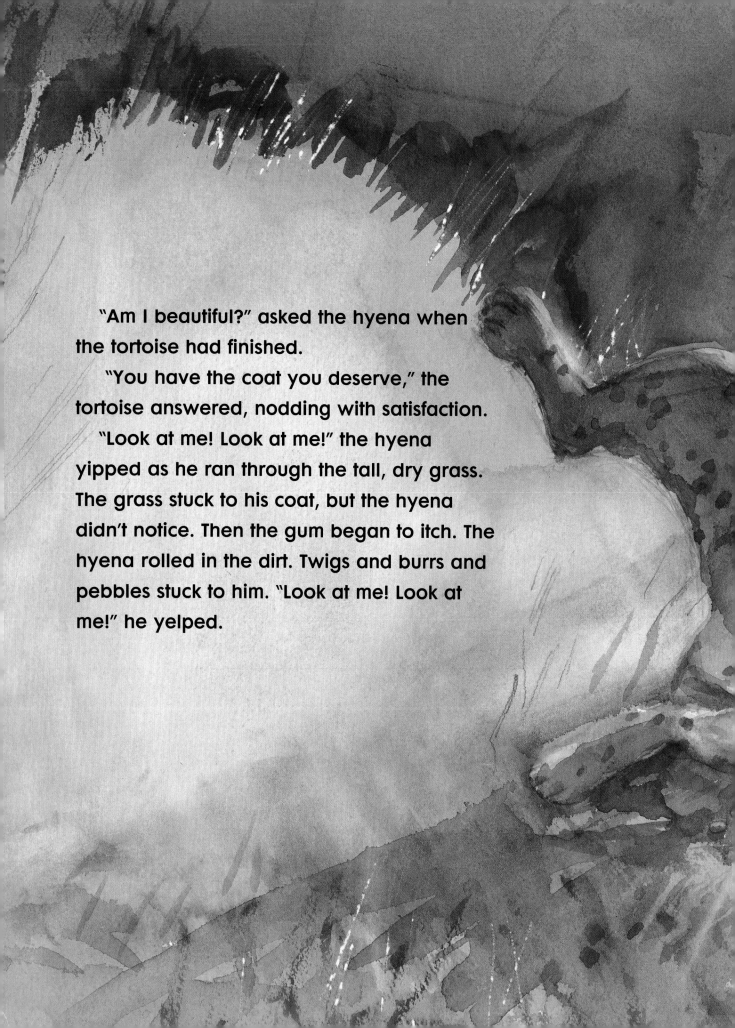

"Am I beautiful?" asked the hyena when the tortoise had finished.

"You have the coat you deserve," the tortoise answered, nodding with satisfaction.

"Look at me! Look at me!" the hyena yipped as he ran through the tall, dry grass. The grass stuck to his coat, but the hyena didn't notice. Then the gum began to itch. The hyena rolled in the dirt. Twigs and burrs and pebbles stuck to him. "Look at me! Look at me!" he yelped.

When he was tired of running, the hyena pranced into the village to show off his new coat. But instead of admiring him, people began to laugh.

"Eh? Am I not beautiful? Like Mbanda? Like Nyalugwe?" he asked. Then he turned his head, and for the first time, he saw his new coat. He looked as beautiful as the garbage heap.

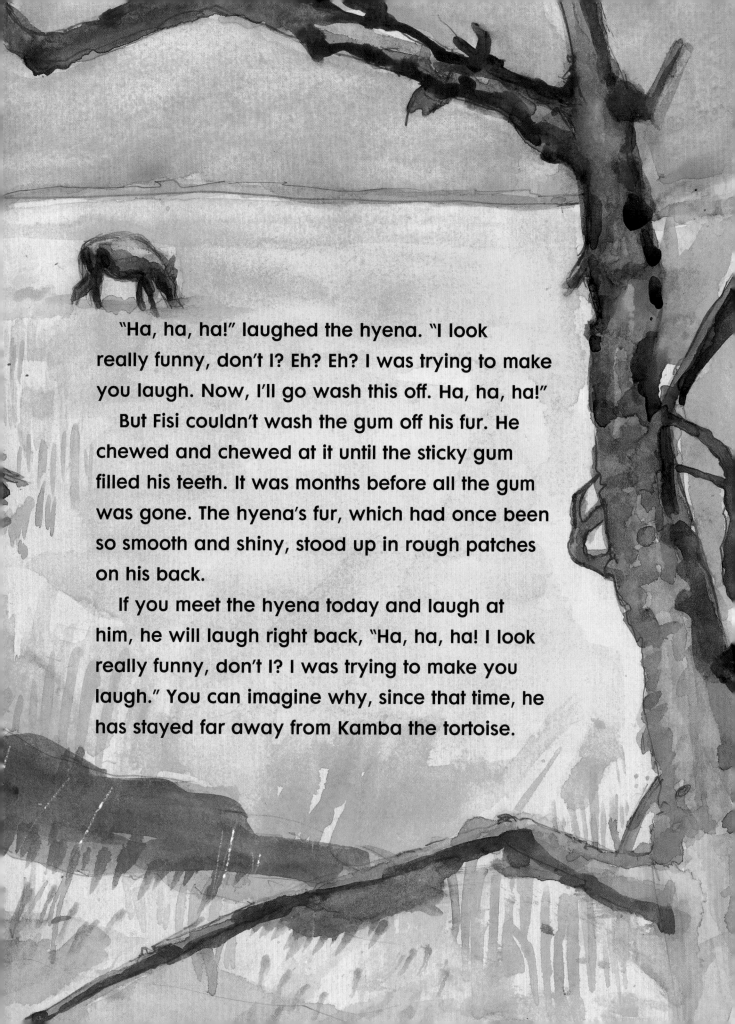

"Ha, ha, ha!" laughed the hyena. "I look really funny, don't I? Eh? Eh? I was trying to make you laugh. Now, I'll go wash this off. Ha, ha, ha!"

But Fisi couldn't wash the gum off his fur. He chewed and chewed at it until the sticky gum filled his teeth. It was months before all the gum was gone. The hyena's fur, which had once been so smooth and shiny, stood up in rough patches on his back.

If you meet the hyena today and laugh at him, he will laugh right back, "Ha, ha, ha! I look really funny, don't I? I was trying to make you laugh." You can imagine why, since that time, he has stayed far away from Kamba the tortoise.

So, you see, don't play a trick on
someone unless you want an even bigger
trick played on you.

Author's Note

This folktale of revenge through art is retold from *Myths and Legends of the Bantu* by Alice Werner. It was originally collected from a storyteller of the Nyanja people, who are the second-largest ethnic group in the country of Malawi. The tale of a tortoise painting animals and destroying the hyena's coat has also been recorded from storytellers in other parts of southern and eastern Africa. Additional details about storytelling traditions of Malawi and the ways and wiles of Kamba and Fisi were gleaned from *Malawian Oral Literature: The Aesthetics of Indigenous Art* by Steve Chimombo. Kamba the tortoise and Fisi the hyena are characters that appear in nearly all the trickster tales of Malawi. According to Dr. Chimombo, Kamba is the slow, steady trickster who is never outwitted, whereas Fisi is the eternal dupe, always tricked and always shamed.